THE MAGI: THE WISE MEN'S JOURNEY TO BABY JESUS

Ken Proctor

Spirit Driven Leadership
spiritdrivenleadership.org

The Magi: The Wise Men's Journey to Baby Jesus
© 2017 Ken Proctor

All rights reserved. This book or any portion thereof may not be reproduced or used in any manner whatsoever without the express written permission of the publisher, except for the use of brief quotations in a book review.

Printed in the United States of America

Book Design: Gary Pool, Shirley de Rose

Spirit Driven Leadership
US Digital Outreach Center
1400 NE 136th Ave
Vancouver WA 98684
www.spiritdrivenleadership.org

Title ID: 7522713
ISBN-13: 978-1975945305
ISBN-10: 1975945301

THE MAGI: THE WISE MEN'S JOURNEY TO BABY JESUS

Bethlehem

The pair came late to the little town. Two weeks they'd been walking, making poor progress on the crowded roads. Their clothing, their hair, even the pores of their exposed skin were encrusted with the fine dust kicked up by grumpy men, haggard wives, exhausted children, overburdened ox carts, donkeys and asses... all the world on the move, for all the world was returning to their roots.

Caesar required a census, which usually meant more taxes, and which entailed everyone returning to their family's point of origin to be counted with their kin. For many, the journey was inconvenient but not terribly long. Homes were locked, shops secured, carts borrowed... they would be back in a week. Two at most. For others, the journey was life altering. Shops were sold, wares discounted or traded, homes abandoned. They might return, eventually... but they might not. Friends parted, partnerships dissolved, couples left in-laws, and wives followed husbands away from the only homes they had ever known.

Push carts, wagons, ox carts and pack frames quickly became scarce, with even the roughest old carriage costing three times its worth. Frustrated buyers haggled fiercely, but the sellers had the advantage. In a few weeks prices would plummet, but for the moment...

The Romans, for their own purposes, have installed their mile markers every one thousand strides along major roads and trade routes. From Nazareth in Galilee to Jerusalem in Judaea, the newly married couple counted over ninety of the stone markers beside the narrow roads that crossed ridges, wound through mountain passes, dropped into valleys, and for the last eighteen miles, climbed over thirty three hundred feet to Jerusalem atop Mount Zion. And they still had over six miles, another day, to go.

So the pair came late to the little town.

✳

It was the innkeeper's wife who first spotted the road weary couple as they walked to the village center and just stopped. Only the man looked about, as his young wife slipped slowly from their donkey's back. With eyes closed and looking inward, the girl leaned against the small beast as the tingling in her feet and legs subsided. The donkey leaned into her weight, and for a moment, with heads nodding, they supported one another.

Watching from her doorway, the innkeeper's wife felt for the pair. The inn was full, and she knew for a fact that every other house, room, shack or hovel for miles about were full, as well. She hated to be the one to disappoint these folks so she prepared to turn away. But then the girl slowly raised one hand to her belly, and the innkeeper's wife recognized that oldest of protective motherly instincts... to shield and comfort the child within.

"With a little work," she thought, "and fresh bedding in the stalls, the empty stable behind the inn will do. Until something better comes available."

Three days later... a star is born.

The Magi: The Wise Men's Journey To Baby Jesus

Egypt

"It has got to be here." In his haste, Gaspar snatched another copper cylinder from the library's storage rack and too quickly tipped the scroll it contained onto the reading desk. He knew he should be more careful with these rare documents, but could not control his rising frustration.

"Gaspar, take care," cautioned his bearded friend. "We will find it when we find it."

"But I just read it a few months ago. No more than half a year at most. I am sure that it was right here in this rack!" The thin man traced his dark index finger over the parchment scroll he has unrolled on the table, looking for a certain passage. He continued scanning it, reading from right to left as he attempted to translate the Aramaic script into his native language in his head.

This challenge was compounded by the fitful light of the candle held by his friend, and fellow scholar, Melchior. During the day, the ancient library was well lit, open and airy, with high timbered ceilings supported by graceful marble columns, vast windows and skylights that illuminated the library, even as its vast collection of books, scrolls, maps, charts, stella, glyphs and tablets illuminated the scholars who flocked here to study and discuss the cumulative knowledge of the known world. But it was no longer day, and only a matter of some urgency had compelled these two to return at such a late hour.

Secondly, the poor and faded condition of the scroll, which was itself a copy of a much older document, forced Gaspar to read much more slowly than his patience would long tolerate. While the world renown Royal Library here at Alexandria was unparalleled both in its architecture and its vast collections of art and literature, its temperate and occasionally humid coastal weather was not well suited to preserving the scrolls themselves. It was a trade off that most scholars accepted, enjoying the comfortable climate in exchange for the necessity to replace old papyri, parchment and rare vellum documents as they aged, faded or rotted.

"No. This isn't the right one either." The aging parchment scroll nearly rolled itself back up as soon as Gaspar released it. He lost more precious minutes rerolling it tight enough to fit back into its cylinder before clunking it back into the rack.

"Patience. Open another... gently, please."

The fourth son of a Persian prince, and therefore a very distant candidate for the throne himself, Melchior had all the advantages of the royal family, including an extensive education and the resources to pursue his interests, but without the royal responsibilities. His current interests included astronomy, astrology and heavenly signs, all of which could best be studied in depth here in Alexandria. Indeed, two hours ago he had been standing with friends on a patio overlooking the shoreline, enjoying a bowl of good Egyptian wine under a clear night sky while watching the last colors of sunset fade into the western sea, when one of the others had pointed to the darker eastern horizon behind them.

"What is that light there, Melchior?" he

had asked. "I'm quite certain that none of the planets is set to rise just yet. Am I mistaken? Or just drunk?" The man looked into his half empty bowl as if to divine the answer there.

Melchior could not at first see what his companion referred to, and was prepared to dismiss the inquiry entirely, when another young scholar also pointed and said, "Yes, I see it. Just rising from the horizon, almost due east."

Stepping into the darker shadow of a nearby column, and hooding his eyes with his hands to block out moonlight and starlight, Melchior focused low on the distant horizon and... there. Yes, a single bright point was ascending from the thin line of haze that frosted the edge of the visible world. But it shouldn't be.

It was early spring, and Virgo would be visible low in the eastern sky from now until late fall, but her stars were well known and this bright point of light on the horizon was right in the middle of Virgo's belly. But it shouldn't be.

Without taking his eyes off the light, Melchior slowly lifted his wine bowl from the patio's stone banister where he had set it a moment before. As he took a long slow drink from it, the raised bowl momentarily eclipsed his view. He closed his eyes, set the bowl aside, cupped his hands to screen out the stars above and looked again at the horizon. Long moments passed before he spoke.

"Gaspar," he had mumbled to himself. "I must find Gaspar."

※

Abandoning his wine, Melchior had hurried through a poorly lit lane to a better lit street. There were three places he might normally expect to find Gaspar: a small and quiet bar, a large and noisy bar, or any bar in between. Gaspar, despite his keen mind, and blinding intellect, was often blind drunk these days. Once away from the restraint of his extensive family in India, and his duties in his father's royal court, his taste for fine wine had quickly deteriorated to include all things fermented.

Melchior was fortunate to spot his

friend in the fourth place he looked, and fortunate, too, that Gaspar had spent more of the evening arguing semantics than actually drinking whatever was set before him.

"Excuse me, gentlemen, for interrupting," Melchior addressed the small group that had gathered about his friend. "I have been sent to fetch your learned companion," he took Gaspar by the elbow and easily hoisted the smaller man to his feet. "His presence is required elsewhere for... uh, for consultation regarding, um, entomology. I bid you good evening." Keeping a firm grip, he began escorting the wriggling and complaining Gaspar toward the door.

"Melchior... ouch! Let me go. I was winning that arg... that debate."

"You were buying the drinks, weren't you?"

"Well, yesss, but..."

"That's why you were winning that debate."

"You are very rude, you know. You should have let me finish my debate and my wine."

"The wine in that place tastes worse

than warm camel piss and you know it. Besides, I need you lucid. We have a mystery to solve."

"A mystery about entomology? You've got the wrong man. I don't know anything about bugs."

"No, a mystery about stars and heavenly signs."

"Oh." Gaspar's attitude changed instantly. "Why didn't you say so?"

"I just did."

"But why didn't you say so to begin with?"

"Because saying so in such a place would arouse far too much interest, and raise far too many questions. We would never have gotten out of there. No one is interested in bugs."

"Patheticus is interested in bugs."

"His name isn't Patheticus. You should stop calling him that."

"Whatever. So, where are you taking me?"

"The main library. The antiquities section. A while back you mentioned something, in passing. Something about a prophecy, a coming king, or kingdom, and a star. You had read something in the library."

"Ya, and as usual, no one was interested. So what?"

"So, now I am interested."

"Why?" Gaspar stopped abruptly. "Why are you suddenly so interested now?" He sounded grumpy and a little hurt.

Melchior had taken a few extra strides before turning to face his friend and colleague. He considered how best to answer the question, then again grabbed his friend by his cloak and hustled him between two buildings toward an open patio overlooking the darkened sea.

"Now, where are we going," Gaspar whined? "I am tired and, if you don't mind, I would like to go to my bed."

Without answering, Melchior dragged him to the far edge of the patio, spun him around to face east and, standing behind him, pointed over Gaspar's shoulder at the far horizon.

"Okay, Melchior. What is the myst..." And then he saw it. "Ooohhh..." Gaspar's own hand rose unbidden to point at the new light that twinkled where the dark night sky met the darker curvature of the sea. "Oh, that's not supposed to be there."

The Magi: The Wise Men's Journey To Baby Jesus

Bethlehem

At first light the next morning, the couple was awakened early by a disturbance outside. The man moved swiftly, snatching up his wooden mallet and stepping lightly to the front of the stable. From the shadow of the doorway, he could see a small crowd gathered in front of the inn, though he could not make out their words. The innkeeper, stepping out to shoo the lot away, became ensnared in the discourse. Minutes ticked by as the group beseeched the proprietor for... for something.

What that something was became clearer when the innkeeper pointed directly at the stable door.

As one, the knot of young men broke away from the innkeeper's door front, and moved toward the stable. Without hesitation, the carpenter stepped into the morning light to defend his wife and her son, but upon seeing his intent, the mob stopped in their tracks. They hadn't anticipated a confrontation.

Instinctively they looked to their

oldest member, a man of perhaps thirty. He, in turn, looked at the carpenter crouched in the doorway, then slowly and deliberately set aside his shepherd's staff, his sling and the small knife from his belt. The others behind him understood, and wordlessly set aside their staffs and anything else that might be considered a weapon. When the shepherd had confirmed that they were all unarmed, he turned again to the man in the door.

"Is there a newborn babe in a manger?" he asked gently. "We were told to look for a babe in a manger."

The mallet fell from the carpenter's hand and he edged aside, as one-by-one the shepherds removed the sandals from their feet before entering.

The Magi: The Wise Men's Journey To Baby Jesus

Egypt

The best way to learn anything required surrounding yourself with the brightest, most intelligent individuals you could find. To that end, Melchior had, upon arriving in the city by the sea, sought out the very brightest minds, sharpest intellects, wisest theologians and most gifted linguists, no matter how uncouth or socially inept they might be, and invited them to dine. In the months that followed, he collected, or rejected, from the thousands of young nobles who had migrated here from all points of the compass to either study or party. Or both. Melchior soon found himself the unofficial leader of an elite core of local and international misfits and gatherings at his spacious accommodations quickly became a weekly tradition. Many among his colleagues had been born to royal lines and dynasties but that heritage had not factored into his winnowing process. In fact, quite a few "members" were the sons of artisans and craftsmen who had been sent, at significant expense to their families, to glean such knowledge or "secrets" as could be applied to enhance that family's craft or trade... and fortunes.

Now, whenever a puzzling question arose, Melchior need not spend days, or even months, nosing through the archives stored in the dry, dusty, hand-hewn tunnels under the main "Royal Library", or the nearby Serapeum Temple Library, or even the Library of the Cesarion Temple across town. He need only turn to one of the many gifted guests at his table and ask. If that scholar did not know the answer, invariably one of the other attendees did. Or knew where to find it quickly. Thereby, all of them contributed to, and benefited from, this co-op of knowledge. A human compendium of nearly encyclopedic information, neatly cross referenced over bread, lamb, lentils and wine.

The information Melchior required just now resided in Gaspar's head. It seemed to be taking longer than usual to extract it, but still far quicker than searching on his own.

"Patience," he repeated. Gaspar was attacking the ribbon which bound another scroll. Perhaps it would be best to wait until the next day to continue the search. With light streaming in through the skylights, and perhaps a few others to help search, assuming the others could translate Aramaic, a little used, nearly archaic language of the Hebrew people.

But something told him this was important, and that time was critical. To whom it was important, or why, he had no clue. Perhaps all would be made clear when Gaspar refound the obscure referen...

"Here!" the little man exclaimed. "I have it. It is right here. See?" His finger pinned the scroll to the desk at a certain place. "Right there." He was grinning now. "I told you I could find it, huh."

"Yes, but what does it say? You know I can't translate that."

"It says, *'The oracle of Balaam, the son of Beor, and the oracle of the man whose eye is opened, the oracle of him who hears the words of God and knows the knowledge of the Most High, and who sees the vision of the Almighty, falling down, yet having his eyes uncovered.'* Melchior, this next part is a quote. *'I see him, but not now; I behold him, but not near; A star shall come forth from Jacob, and a scepter shall rise from Israel, and shall crush the forehead of Moab, and undermine all the sons of Seth. And Edom shall be a possession, Seir, its enemies, also shall be a possession, while Israel performs valiantly. One from Jacob shall have dominion and shall destroy the remnant from the city.'"*

The two men stood over the scroll in silence for a long moment before Melchior spoke. "So what does it..."

"I have no idea," Gaspar interrupted. "Just because I can read this, doesn't mean I know what it means. The first part is obviously an introduction to the second part, and the second part is obviously prophetic and refers to an individual in the future. But beyond that...? The person we need to..."

"Balthasar," inserted Melchior.

"Yes. Balthasar may know."

※

Balthasar had slept in evidently, and

high noon had passed before Melchior could get past Omid, his diligent steward.

"Melchior, my friend, you have saved me a walk across town to bid you farewell and good fortune."

"What? You are going somewhere?" In his haste, Melchior had not noticed that many furnishings were missing, to be replaced by light chests, hampers, bundles and wicker baskets. Balthasar's household was packing to leave.

"Home," answered the charismatic Arab with a grin. It was not often that his friend the Persian prince was caught off guard like this. "My mind and my eyes are filled to overflowing with the wonders of this place, but my heart is now heavy with thoughts of home. It is overlong since my sojourn here began, though my good friends have made the time pass quickly. None the less, with regret, I must embark soon for home. Surely you understand."

"Yes... of course... its just that a certain matter has arisen. I... we need your council regarding a prophecy." Melchior hoped not to reveal too much until they could speak in private.

"Ah. I see. You've seen the star, then." A statement, not a question.

"You know about the..?"

"Certainly. I was up half the night staring at it and considering the implications. The only prophecy I can recall that might relate to this appearance pertains to a coming king in Palestine."

"Yes, Gaspar and I found the text of the prophecy in a parchment scroll he recalled reading months ago. He was able to translate the words but the meaning is obscure. We had hoped that you could help us interpret it. When were you planning to depart?"

"In another week, perhaps. Ten days at most. Certainly before the heat of summer. Gaspar was sober enough to..?"

"He was fine. Is fine," Melchior answered a bit too quickly. Balthasar thought he sounded defensive, but let it go. He knew that Melchior would just as readily defend the honor of any among his circle of friends. Including Balthasar's. "Very well then. Between now and the moment I depart for home, I am at your disposal, provided we meet here. Omid will supervise packing, provisioning and preparations, but I must remain nearby to supervise Omid."

"I accept," the Persian answered, then added, "You will be missed, my friend. How shall we find an intellect to replace yours at my table?"

"Can't be done," the Arab scholar grinned back. "No point in trying." The two friends shared a laugh and a back-slapping hug. Both men ranked low enough among their respective royal lines to set politics aside and find a kinship, a brotherhood among fellow scholars in an academic environment.

"The book is titled 'In the Wilderness', or 'While in the Wilderness', and records the dealings of the Hebrew God with that nation centuries ago," reported Gaspar, "but based on what I have translated so far, if I had been their god, I would have smitten the whole rebellious, ungrateful lot of them with... well, with something unpleasant, and been done with them."

"Do not be so hasty to judge them, my friend," chided Balthasar. "The same god is the source of the prophecy we now hope to divine."

Gathering that evening at Balthasar's residence, the three men scanned a copy of the prophecy that Gaspar had translated into Greek.

"Shall we take it line by line, then?" suggested Melchior.

"Yes, but skip the flowery introduction," added Gaspar.

"*I see him, but not now; I behold him but not near...*'" read Balthasar. "So we have a prophecy regarding a man at some point in the future. *'A star shall come forth from Jacob, and a scepter shall rise from Israel...'* The star appears to hold a double meaning. The star is the man coming forth from the lineage of Jacob, and the star is just a star, but it rises out of, or over, the land of Jacob."

"Who is Jacob?" Melchior wanted to know. "And the land of Jacob, where would that be?"

"The short answer is 'Israel'", said

Gaspar.

"Israel is the short answer to what?"
"Your question."
"Which one?"
"Both."

"Perhaps," interjected Balthasar, "you should give us a longer answer, Gaspar."

"Fine. Jacob is Israel. The land of Jacob is the land of Israel."

"Longer, Gaspar, and remember what I did the last time you tried our patience." Balthasar was not smiling. He tolerated the Indian's idiosyncrasies for Melchior's sake, but he had his limits.

"According to related histories and genealogies, Jacob fathered twelve sons, and all of them and their families emigrated to Egypt hundreds of years ago. You both remember the stories of the plagues visited upon Egypt in the reign of Ramses the First, right? Jacob's people became a huge nation while in Egypt and, following the plagues, they left to go back home to Palestine. Well they got side- tracked along the way and ended up wandering around in the Sinai, the Wilderness of Etham, the Wilderness of Zin, the Wilderness of Paran, the hill country of Middian and the plains of Edom. Hence the name of the book."

"And this prophecy is written in the book about that time wandering in the wilderness?"

"Yes."

"Which brings us back to my original question," Melchior said. "Who was Jacob and why do you say he was Israel?"

"His father, a man named Isaac, named him Jacob. However," he held up a finger to silence Balthasar, who was visibly losing his composure, "however, their god changed his name to Israel, which translates as "he fights with God," or "he wrestles with God."

"Okay, so... back to the prophecy," said Melchior, trying to get the discussion back on track. "*A star shall come forth from Jacob*, which is Israel, and *a scepter shall rise out of Israel*, which is the land of Jacob."

"The scepter is an obvious reference to royalty," said Balthasar. "So we could deduce that a man who will be a king will be born to the lineage of Jacob, also known as Israel, and a star will rise over the land of Israel."

"And now," interjected Melchior, "a new star appears, rising low on the horizon due east of here. And what is due east of here? Palestine. The land of Israel."

"So what?" Gaspar asked rhetorically, "princes are born every day. You are a prince, and you are a prince. Even I am a prince. Half the students in this city are princes, or nobility of some sort. But..." and here he paused for effect, "would you like to know what else I found?"

Melchior had to step between Balthasar and Gaspar before the former could throttle the latter. "What else did you find?" he asked.

"Another prophecy." Gaspar was obviously pleased with himself and gloating.

"Don't make us ask again, my friend," said Melchior.

"Don't make me pin you to an ant hill," snarled Balthasar.

"Last night, while looking for this prophecy, I read another in a separate scroll, but from the same rack. It also was in Aramaic and was part of a larger compilation of..."

"Gaspar," growled Balthasar.

"Patience, my surly friend," soothed

Melchior. "Get to the point, please, Gaspar. What was this second prophecy?"

"Okay, the Hebrew prophet Isaiah records this prophecy: *'Therefore, the Lord Himself will give you a sign; behold a virgin shall conceive, and bear a son, and shall call his name Immanuel, which is 'God with us.'*"

No one spoke for a moment.

"And you think this is related because...?"

"In which constellation did the new star appear?" Gaspar loved rhetorical questions. "Virgo," he answered himself.

Balthasar bade them move the discussion to a bright, airy courtyard, seated them on padded benches and called for watered wine, dates and bread. They now had two prophecies to deal with, but these men were guests in his house and they might as well be comfortable.

"But are the two related?" Melchior asked. "Perhaps we should finish dissecting the first passage before complicating matters with the second."

"But, theoretically," argued Gaspar, "both come from the same source, the Hebrew god, whatever His name is. They never write it down."

"And both refer to the birth of a son," added Balthasar. "In the first, the son becomes a king, but in the second, he either becomes a god, or is born a god."

"They only have one god." They all knew this. It was one of the things that made those people peculiar among the other nations. "So," Melchior extrapolated, "if they only have the one, and this prophecy is from The One, and about The One, then the son of the virgin must *be* The One."

"But does it follow that this star is a marker related to that specific prophecy?" challenged Balthasar. "Not necessarily. Based on what we know, we cannot assume that the two prophecies are related."

"Neither can we assume that they are not," countered Gaspar.

"Again," offered Melchior, "we simply do not have enough information upon which to decide that question. Getting back to the original prophecy, Gaspar, what comes after the scepter?"

"That portion is more difficult to translate; several of the words can have multiple meanings depending on the context. For instance, where it is written, '...*and shall crush through the forehead of Moab*' it could be translated, *and shall conquer the corners, or the borders, of Moab*, which changes the meaning somewhat. Likewise the next line, '...*tear down all the sons of Sheth*,' could as easily be translated, *undermine the sons of Sheth*, which would be everyone in the world, or *the sons of Heth*, which would be the Hittites, or *the sons of Seth*, who are the Caananites."

"That is not particularly helpful," grumped Balthasar.

"I am sorry, but to be more clear you will need to dig up a five hundred year old Hebrew scribe who understands the nuance of the language, culture and dialect common to that period."

"Or go find out for ourselves," Melchior added, glibly. He was staring blankly at a wall over Gaspar's left shoulder. Already his mind was elsewhere. this line of questioning was leading them nowhere, but he did not know where else to look. Interpreting prophecy had never been a talent he desired, or an interest he had pursued. He had pinned his hopes on his Arab friend's reputed expertise in this area, but Balthasar had provided only limited illumination.

"Okay," said Balthasar. "It is not far out of my way."

"What is? Or isn't, rather? Far out of your way?" Melchior felt he had missed something.

"Palestine, of course. I had planned to join my entourage to the next trade caravan heading east along the roads toward home, but if you like, we could take the northern route through Gaza, then Marisa and on to Jerusalem.

"What... who is we, and why are you going to Jerusalem?"

"We is you and me, and if there is a king born in Palestine, it would probably be in Jerusalem."

"Who said anything about going to

Jerusalem," Melchior gasped?

"You did," the other two stated in unison.

"You said we should all go find out for ourselves," added Gaspar.

"He wasn't talking about you, Gaspar. You can't come."

"Why not?"

"Because you are annoying. It is my trip, my caravan, my rules. Melchior needs to come, but you don't."

"You need me." Gaspar pointed out.

"Why?"

"Because neither of you understands Hebrew or Aramaic," the Indian answered with a self-satisfied smirk. "And I do."

✷

Melchior felt his tidy world was spinning out of control. With less than a week to prepare for the planned departure, he had much to do. Still unclear how he'd managed to get included on this quest to Palestine, the others assured him that it had been his idea all along.

"But it is over three hundred Roman miles," he had explained, hoping to discourage them.

"Three hundred miles if we went by sea directly to Gaza and overland from there," noted Gaspar.

"Which we are not," corrected Balthasar. "Traveling overland along the coast road, then north and east to Jerusalem will be closer to three hundred and fifty of the Romans' miles. About four weeks, if we are lucky. Longer if we are not."

"How will we find the new king once we get there?" Melchior persisted. "We don't really know where to begin looking. Or what to look for."

"We can begin in Jerusalem. Surely someone there can direct us to whichever palace the child was born in. The birth of a royal prince would not be kept a secret. No doubt royal envoys from many nations will be arriving to extend official congratulations."

"Or," Gaspar suggested, "we could just follow the star."

Melchior and Balthasar had blinked and

actually considered the idea before Balthasar took off his sandal and threw it at Gaspar.

※

Melchior's household was much simpler than Balthasar's. Only two personal servants and five household servants, including the cook. Still, the logistics of preparing to decamp from his rented accommodations and pack provisions for the long trip were exhausting. And it was remarkable the amount of stuff he had accumulated in the few years he had resided in Alexandria.

In the end, Melchior donated quite a number of documents to one library or another and either sold or gave the heavier furnishings to his many friends and colleagues. He converted silver coins into the smaller gold coins, or used it to purchase expensive spices and resins, like murrha and olibanum, which were much lighter, yet easily converted back to coin as need arose.

He still had grave reservations about this journey, but with one day to spare before leaving the city by the sea, Melchior felt prepared. He stood in his nearly empty residence and looked at the blank walls, the empty corners, and asked himself again, "Why am I leaving?" A voice behind him made him jump.

"Because I asked," repeated Balthasar. "Are you doubting your decision?"

"It feels like the decision was made for me, and rather quickly, but no. Now that I have resolved to seek answers there to the questions raised here... no, I have no reservations. A few regrets perhaps. I have been content here, and will miss the company of so many brilliant men. And the few I count as friends. But it is time to return to my father's house and this quest provides a good pretext for taking the first steps toward home. It is time."

"It is time," Balthasar agreed. "We leave at first light."

ns’ Journey To Baby Jesus

Bethlehem

The young carpenter soon had the inn's stable as comfortable as a small house. His gifted hands, along with the tools he had carried on his back from home, would be their sole source of income.

The innkeeper, brow beaten by his wife into allowing the pair to use the space, was pleasantly surprised at the improvements to the structure, and shortly after the babe was born, engaged the young carpenter in repairs to the inn. Then, having purchased used carts and wagons from some of his out-of-town guests, he had the young father make repairs to those, as well.

On the eighth day, in accordance with the law and customs of their people, the carpenter presented the boy to the local priest, that he be named and circumcised.

After a few weeks, a modest one-room house became available in town and the carpenter moved his wife and the boy there. Though still considered outsiders, largely on account of their subtle, but distinctive, northern dialect and accents, the two were quickly becoming accepted by the tiny community. The census insured that, for the moment, everyone in town was related to everyone else, so the young couple and their infant son were considered long lost relatives. Now, having seen the young man's skills, and the young couples need, more offers of work came his way. The remarkable tale the shepherds had told didn't hurt either.

The Magi: The Wise Men's Journey To Baby Jesus

Egypt

"If he is late, we are leaving without him," declared Balthasar. "The caravan leader will not wait."

"He will be here," Melchior assured the normally amiable Arab. "I spoke with him just last night and he assured me." Despite his confident words, Melchior again scanned back along the road to the city gates, hoping to spot Gaspar rushing to join them.

Most trade coming to Alexandria arrived by boat or barge, either along the coast or down the western-most branch of the Nile. This small caravan, a mixed lot of merchants, spice traders, camel mongers and assorted travelers who had joined for the relative safety of traveling with others, had arrived from the west, following the coast roads and skirting between the sea and the northern edge of the great desert. They were traveling light and fast, laden only with animal hides to trade and provisions for the journey. The caravan's destination was the port city of Memphis on the Nile River. Once there, they would restock, purchasing spices, ivory, silk, gems, tin, iron bars, copper ingots and other luxury items, all of which had been transported by others from much further east. The endless cycle of the trade route.

Having rested the beasts while concluding such trading as was available here, the caravan members were anxious to set out in the cool of the day. They would rest again in the heat of each day, and then travel again until near night fall. The sooner they followed the western Nile southeast to Memphis, the sooner they could turn again west with fresh goods. Already the caravan leader was mounted on his horse and deploying the line of beasts and men.

Balthasar's troop would join the other assorted travelers in the midst of the line. His entourage included his steward, Omid, twelve various servants and staff, and twenty four beasts, mostly camels, although for his personal use he had purchased a fine horse. The remainder of his household, local servants, a tailor, two cooks and a stable boy had been dismissed, and promptly rehired to serve in the same residence by its new tenant.

By contrast, Melchior had retained only his two personal servants, each riding a camel and leading two others laden with provisions. Besides food for themselves and grain for the camels, skins of water were suspended from each animals saddle or pack frame. A modest tent and bedding for himself, and a second to cover their provisions at night, were strapped to the top of two loads. The balance of his baggage consisted of clothing, personal items and six books that would double his father's modest private collection. Gifts for his father, and for the king, would be purchased much closer to home to spare the beasts the extra weight.

As the leading elements of the camel train formed up and took to the road, Melchior watched as his people made one last inspection of each beast and burden, snugging straps and lanyards. Mounting up, they moved to join Balthasar, whose own people were preparing to join the march.

The noise of camel herders and travelers getting their beasts on their feet, mixing with the bellowed replies from irritable creatures, presented a stark contrast to the relatively peaceful sanctuary of the scholarly world he had grown accustomed to, and once again he wondered if this impulsive trip had been a wise or prudent choice. They weren't even on the main trail yet and already his tail bone was protesting. He made a mental note to purchase a fleece from one of the traders, and use it to pad his saddle until his body had adapted to this new form of abuse.

"I have arrived," called a cheery voice behind him. Melchior, roused from his inward thoughts, turned in the saddle and saw Gaspar... riding in an open-sided sedan chair strapped securely to the back of the biggest bull camel he had ever seen, and flanked by two servants, each mounted on a female camel, with a third man leading the way.

"Do you like it?" the Indian prince asked. "I had it custom made. Very comfortable, yes?" A broad, fringed, cotton canopy, suspended on four slender poles provided its grinning rider shade, and numerous tassels along its edges shooed away pesky flies as they swayed with the rhythm of the animals pace. Thick cushions and a well padded back rest insured the rider's comfort.

"My father has a similar chair back in India," Gaspar explained, "but of course, his is much larger and mounted on an elephant." Balthasar had noticed the commotion and spurred his horse back toward them. As he pulled up along side Melchior, he just shook his head. "What is that... that contraption, Gaspar?"

"It is called a sedan chair. Very nice, yes?"

"It looks like a hairy brothel on four legs."

"How do you steer it?" Melchior wanted to know. "Your camel has no reins or lead ropes."

"That is not a problem. You see that camel in front of mine," asked Gaspar? "That camel is his mother. Where she goes he follows. Simple." The Indian prince grinned. He was very pleased with himself.

Balthasar shot Melchior a look that said, *'I told you bringing him along was a bad idea,'* and rode off to rejoin his band. Melchior took a second to confirm that his troop was falling in behind the others before turning again to Gaspar.

"Where is the rest of your baggage?" The young Persian had expected to be the smallest party among the three comrades, yet Gaspar's three men had only the parcels strapped behind their own saddles, and few extra beasts in tow.

"Unlike you and Balthasar, I will be returning to the comforts of Alexandria, so most of my belongings are still there in the care of my steward. Since we will be traveling up the coast road and passing through Gaza, I made arrangements to ship provisions to a trusted agent in that city. We will restock as needed along the way. And once we have concluded this venture, I plan to caravan back to Gaza or some other port city, sell the beasts and secure passage by boat back here. Simple."

"But you don't even have a tent." Melchior liked the brilliant and eccentric young Indian, but did not relish sharing his tent with the man. And there was no way Balthasar was likely to offer space in his pavilion. "Where do you plan to sleep?"

Gaspar's grin got impossibly wide as he reached forward to pull a cord. With a soft 'flap', four sides dropped from the sedan's canopy, unfurling to totally screen the rider from view. And from flying insects. Melchior could hear his friend laughing beyond the veil, and could only shake his head as the laughter turned to song. For all the man's brilliance, he could not carry a tune.

⁕

At Memphis, as expected, the caravan disbanded. Those going back west with trade goods would leave again in a matter of days. Those proceeding on had to ferry their beasts and belongings across the Nile to Heliopolis, further down river on the eastern side. Once there, it took almost a week before they could join, for a modest fee, a suitable caravan headed northeast, following the established routes through the lush, low delta lands called Goshen, across the northern edge of Sinai, and along the coastal plains of Philistia to Gaza where they would rest and resupply.

The next two hundred miles, though fairly flat and level, would still take over two weeks. It could be done faster if haste was required, but the heavily laden beasts would be useless by the time they got there.

To spare both his camel and his tail bone, Melchior often walked. Still young and, for a royal scholar, fairly fit, the exercise was no challenge. He also found that walking was beneficial with regard to his digestion. Trail food, he had discovered, could be difficult to pass.

Walking also made it easier to chat with others along the way, and opened for him a whole other realm of education that had been missing in the sterile halls of academia: the world of average men and women, ordinary folks who had developed specialized skills in order to secure a living for themselves and their families. With his royal robes and regal trappings safely stored away, he often passed himself off as an advisor or emissary to some distant potentate, and simply listened and learned the life lessons of the "little people".

By observing the various merchants and tradesmen, he learned several ways to evenly distribute a camel's load and to secure it with various knots. He was taught other useful knots for staking tents, for lashing a broken pack frame, and for snaring a desert hare for dinner. Once the merchants had warmed to him, they expounded at length on how to judge cotton, taste wine, grade rubies and cut off a thief's fingers. One ugly camel herder generously offered to explain how to assess the health of a camel by tasting its droppings.

There was so much to know, so much to learn... from people who could not read a book. Assuming they ever saw one. Gaspar had been observed reading through scrolls while happily ensconced in his high chair, and the superstitious common folk avoided him. Reading was like magic, and magic was not of this world. It didn't help matters when his servants, sensing the unease of their peers, began spreading little rumors about what magic the books contained, and how powerful the man in the chair was. When Melchior discovered their game, he tried to quash it, but the damage was done. Nothing spreads as fast as juicy gossip fueled by fear of the unknown.

Between lessons on camel breeding,

sandal mending and the culinary vagaries of the local flora and fauna, Melchior attempted to glean any information or gossip these folks might have picked up regarding a new prince born to the nation of Israel. The first thing he learned was that that kingdom was now called Judaea, and encompassed most of the lands between the Jordan River and the Great Sea, from Galilee in the north, to Moab in the south.

Secondly, the current king was named Herod, and though he had a number of sons, no one could recall any sons, or grandsons, born recently. In fact, during his long reign Herod was reputed to have executed or assassinated one wife, three of his sons and two or three son-in-laws. Though considered a masterful politician and a great builder of public works, his jealousy and paranoia were famous, as well. And potentially lethal.

Thirdly, though the fairly flat terrain they were passing through allowed them to view the new star most nights, when ask about it these common folk just shrugged. Stars did not put coins in their pockets or food on their tables, assuming they stayed in one place long enough to justify owning a table.

※

Melchior leaned on the low table in Balthasar's tent.

"The more I learn about King Herod..."

"Yes," agreed Balthasar, "I see your point. We will need to be very cautious in dealing with him."

"Dealing with him? It might be wiser to avoid him entirely."

"If we cannot discover the boy king on our own between now and then, we must inquire at the royal court. And having inquired, it would be considered unthinkably rude to not pay our respects to the king. So if we are bound to seek an audience with Herod anyway, we might as well seek his guidance regarding the prophecies. Whether it is wise or safe or prudent or madness, we will probably stand before the king eventually. And we will need to be prepared."

"Prepared how?" asked Melchior.

"First, in order for Herod to take us

seriously, he must see that we are royalty. We must dress like princes, act like princes and speak like princes, like future kings, if we are to be seen as his near equal.

"Second, we should ask only nonspecific questions, pretending to know less than we do so that, having answered our questions, Herod will feel superior and look good in his own eyes for having known something that we did not. Likewise we should be generous with our praise and offer some small service in return."

"And thirdly?" asked Melchior.

"Thirdly, having learned all we can with regard to the prophecies and the star, we find the child to confirm those prophecies and then go on home. If we can accomplish all that we hoped for, it will make for a good story to tell my family and my king. Imagine... we might find the son of the Hebrew god, the future king of the Jews."

"We would be famous," exclaimed a voice from the front of the tent. Gaspar parted the front door flaps and let himself in. "Famous in song and story. Little children will beg to here the story retold for centuries to come, the story of the three princes who marched into Herod's court and got themselves killed for trying to find the child who would usurp Herod's throne. Are you two crazy?"

"That is why I did not invite you to my tent, Gaspar. You do not understand the nuances of diplomacy in the courts of kings. Yes, if we go stomping in and demand to see the next king of the Jews, we may find ourselves impaled on a pointy stake hoping to die sooner rather than later; however, with tact, charm and discretion, all of which you lack, Gaspar, we can make our inquiries look harmless, even helpful to the king." Turning to Melchior, he added, "Is it too late to send him back to Alexandria? Perhaps drop him off at Gaza and let him sail back early?"

"Have you learned to translate Hebrew or Aramaic?"

"No."

"Then be nice to Gaspar. He means well and we require his aid."

"Then I shall pray to the Hebrew god that we find the child king before it is necessary to call on the old king for his assistance."

"You don't even know their god's

name," pointed out Gaspar.

"That's okay," said Balthasar, "He does."

✦

While the trade route hugged the Nile's delta through the lands of Goshen, water remained abundant and readily available. But within the week, the trail turned east again, crossing a nearly flat and featureless arid strip to Lake Bullah. Once they passed Lake Bullah, however, and entered the wilderness call Shur, the next opportunity to fill their water skins and water their beasts would be the stream known to the locals as Wadi al Arish, and by the Hebrews as Nahal Mitzrayim, "the brook of Egypt"... about 90 miles away beyond the wilderness.

The princes had allowed two weeks to get from Memphis to Gaza, hoping to average fourteen to fifteen miles per day. In reality, however, the ancient trade route was not as direct as the library's maps had indicated, often looping upstream or downstream as travelers sought a place to ford a river or dry wadi. Or having to negotiate through swampy lowlands and detour around herds of wild buffalo.

They lost nearly half of one day at the great portage road where cargo passing up the Red Sea was transported overland to reach the Mediterranean by way of the Nile. And visa-versa. Often, the vessels themselves were partially dismantled and hauled on great carts, to be reassembled at the end of the trail. As the three princes awaited an opportunity to safely cross the two-way traffic, one small ship, dragged intact by great teams of oxen, passed before them.

"Why has no one thought to dig a canal here?" Balthasar wondered, aloud. "Surely it would be faster, simpler and cheaper to pay a fee for passage, than to deal with this portage."

"It has been tried," answered Gaspar, the historian of the three. "Several times, actually. The details are boring but three factors mitigated against it: the sands of the desert kept filling in the great trench so it had to be redug constantly; it was discovered that the Red Sea is slightly higher than the Nile at the point of connection and would foul the fresh irrigation water down stream; and thirdly... them," he said, pointing to all the men carting goods and dragging loads along the sun-baked earthen road.

"What about them?" asked Melchior, though he suspected the answer.

"Portaging is big business, and fairly profitable. A canal would put most of them out of business. Likewise, those businesses pay fees, or taxes, or both to Pharaoh. So, with no effort or investment of his own, he receives a share of their profits. Why build a complicated canal?"

※

Melchior did the math in his head. Ultimately, it had taken nine days just to get from the port of Memphis trekking northeast along the eastern fork of the Nile and then east to Lake Bullah, averaging less than nine miles per day. At that rate, it would take another nine days to reach the banks of the river Mitzrayim on the northern border of Egypt, and another four or five to arrive at Gaza. Almost a week behind schedule.

"I hope we have enough supplies," Melchior mumbled to himself. There were no towns or villages along this stretch. He turned in the saddle looking back along the trail. Lake Bullah had already faded into the distance. His water skins were full. But would they last?

On the third day out from Bullah, the wind shifted. At first, many of the travelers barely noted the calm, but by midday a steady hot, dry wind blowing up off the desert interior had replaced the mild, slightly humid breezes from the temperate sea to the north.

To Melchior, it was evident that the traders and herdsmen who passed this way on a regular basis were not happy. They looked at the sky off to their right, glanced at the sun above, studied the trail ahead, and then looked at their feet and kept walking. Melchior, dismounting to walk for a while, approached the herdsman who had taught him to set snares.

"Some of us do not look happy this morning," he commented, pointing to several other camel herders. The man glanced again off toward the inhospitable interior, shrugged and focused again on the trail before his feet. Melchior respected his silence, slowing just a bit to let the man move off. He saw Gaspar in his sedan, the papyrus scroll he was trying to read kept fluttering in the rising wind and, eventually, he gave up, focusing instead on keeping various cushions from blowing away.

The horizon off over the desert interior became less distinct, turning from clear blue to a light, sandy haze. A commotion ahead caught his attention. Balthasar was trotting his horse along the line of march, shouting instructions to his people. Melchior took a minute to have his camel kneel so he could remount, then hurried forward to talk to the Arab who was still giving orders.

"If that gets close," Balthasar said, pointing at the growing haze on the horizon, "there will not be time to set up the tents. Use your camels as shields. They will know to lie down together. You must cover yourselves and huddle behind the beasts. Sleep if you can but do not get up until the storm is over." His friend moved off again before the Persian could thank him.

Turning off the trail, Melchior allowed his camel to grab a quick snack off some light brush while he waited for his own little band to catch up. To stretch the limited feed they had packed, all the beasts were allowed to graze on whatever could be found along the way, which at this point wasn't much.

In the wild, the camels could subsist on nearly nothing for weeks, living off the reserve of fat stored in their fleshy humps, but packing heavy loads over long distances required a more steady and nutritious diet. He made a mental note to give his little herd some grain later. And water. He looked once more to the indistinct horizon and then turned the reluctant animal back toward the trail. They would trek on as far as possible today. If the storm came, it came.

It came. By late afternoon, with unbelievable suddenness, the dry breeze from the south turned to a gusting, dust laden wind. Instinctively, the camels sought out the thin lines of brush, low gravely dunes or rocky outcrops behind which to lie down. There was no time to unload them, but Melchior had insured that robes and tarps were ready at hand and each of them snuggled in the lee of a camel, tucking the loose ends of tarps beneath themselves.Trapped in this make shift shelter, he fully appreciated how bad the camel smelled. Or perha ps it was himself.

※

The sun rose bright and clear but the caravan was a shambles. A number of camels, not properly staked for the night, had wandered off in search of fodder. A few others, evidently, had disappeared along with two of the herdsmen, the opportunity to make off with valuable beasts and baggage under the cover of the storm proving too tempting.

Melchior took stock of his situation.

His men and his beasts were accounted for and had weathered the wind storm without loss, but without sleep, too. One of their water skins had burst when a camel lay down on it. The other skins were sound and Melchior passed one around so they could clear their throats of dust. The camels could smell the water and nosed between the men looking for a drink. A drink, along with half an ohmer of grain, was all they each got; they would have to wait for the river ahead to truly slake their thirst.

"I need a bath." Gaspar had walked over from his 'camp' and stood brushing dust from his robe and then bent over to tossle the grit from his hair. "Who's idea was this anyway?" He did not expect an answer and did not wait for one. "We should have booked passage on a barge or boat. We would have been in Gaza by now."

"Yes, and paying top dollar both for the boatsmen and for camels once we reached the coast of Philistia. Neither of us could afford that and Balthasar is transporting quite a lot of people and goods."

"There are big boats," Gaspar grumped.

He had to get the last word. Melchior decided to let him and changed the subject.

"I can be ready to leave here in an hour. Will you be ready?"

"That depends," Gaspar answered while continuing to shake fine sand from the folds of his cloak.

"Depends on what?"

"How quickly my servants can locate my cushions. When Jobo laid down, my sedan tipped over. I rolled out and my cushions went flying. Literally. I cannot ride without cushions."

"Who is Jobo?"

"My camel, of course. I had to call him something." The young Indian prince put his hat back on, then changed his mind and used the hat to beat more dust from his cloak. "I cannot be ready in an hour," he added. "It will take hours to clean all of the sand from the baggage. It managed to get into everything except my little tin of tea."

"Then we will see you in Gaza when you catch up." Melchior moved off to help his men finish packing and checking the loads. He knew lack of sleep was affecting his ability to deal with his friend, but at this point he didn't care. He needed a bath, too, but he and the camels would not get what they needed until they reached the river, and the sooner they got moving, the sooner they got there.

But that was a week away.

※

They lingered a day beside the Mitzrayim, having forded the shallow stream the day before. It would likely be reduced to a dry wadi by the height of summer but proved a welcome respite now. Water skins were filled before they crossed, and the camels all stopped midstream to drink their fill. Once camp was established, nearly everyone took time to wash themselves and relax. Before dark, the camels were allowed again to drink their fill and browse on the relatively lush growth along the banks.

The day of rest was needed. By unspoken consensus, no one bothered to rise early or strike camp. A day was needed to rest the animals, rinse out their travel stained clothing, bathe again in the tepid water and mend worn sandals and tack. At midday, Melchior had dined with Balthasar before returning to his own extinguished fire to sleep through the heat of the day.

"Four days," the caravan master had answered. Melchior had hailed him as he passed by the next morning while getting everyone in order for the days march. "We are rested, we have plenty of water, and the road beyond here is fairly level and straight. If we press forward, we can be in Gaza in four more days. Five at most." The man did not linger to engage in conversation. Not the talkative type.

The trade route they were following hugged the coastline, arching gently northward. It followed the Mediterranean all the way north past Gaza, Ashdod, Joppa and Tyre to far off Arvad, a port city in northern Phoenicia, before turning east into the fertile crescent... Persia... 'home,' thought

Melchior. But for now, he would be content to finish crossing this sandy plain and rejoin civilization at Gaza, in Philistia.

"What do we know of the Philistines," he asked Gaspar. They had been riding abreast on the second morning out from their rest stop on the river, and discussing various topics including agriculture, philosophy, and the merits of goat cheese over yak or buffalo cheese. Much of the ornate sedan chair had been lost in the storm, along with many of the bolsters and cushions. The cotton sunroof, along with the side veils, had been the first to go, so Gaspar had adopted a broad brimmed hat, more practical than stylish. Or regal.

"Very cultured. Highly advanced. No doubt they prefer goat cheese... like me. Why do you ask?"

"Do you speak their language?"

"Of course. So do you."

"I do?" Melchior asked, turning to look to see if his friend was joking. He wasn't.

"Historically, the Philistines are seafarers and traders. As I understand it, they migrated by sea from the Ionian Peninsula to the coast of Canaan, established trade outposts and eventually, as sailors are apt to do, married local girls, adopted local customs and picked up some of the language. But if you speak Greek, which you do, you can get by."

"Are they hostile?"

"Only to the Hebrews. They've been squabbling over territory for generations, centuries in fact. The five cities of Philistia are organized as independent city states, like they had back in Ionia, but when they aren't feuding with each other, they join ranks against outside threats. Gaza is one of those city states, and the Hebrews are currently their primary outside threat. You weren't planning to ask around Gaza about a new child born King of the Jews, were you?"

"Well I assumed that, since they are neighbors..."

"I wouldn't suggest it. Remember those pointy stakes we talked about trying to avoid in Jerusalem? I'm sure they know how to sharpen a stake in Gaza, too."

Melchior rode in silence for a while. *'How did this get so complicated?'* he wondered to himself. It had all begun as a mystery, an academic research project, involving a star that appears from nowhere, in a place it shouldn't be, that may or may not relate to an ancient prophecy, written in a musty old scroll, in an archaic language, from a god with no name, about the birth of Himself.

"It started out complicated," he muttered to himself.

"If you are speaking to me, you must speak up," said Gaspar.

Melchior didn't answer.

'So how do we find the truth?' he asked himself. *'Find the child?'*

He steered his camel around another traveler who had stopped in the middle of the trail to adjust a load.

'And how do we find the child?' He scratched at an itchy spot on his scalp.
'We ask for directions.'

'Who knows about the child and can direct us to him?'

'His parents know, of course, but presumably they are together, so if we find the parents, we find the child.'

'Who else knows?'

'If the star is truly a sign, the Hebrew scholars must know.'

'Where are the scholars?'

'Presumably in the king's court.'

'So we still must seek an audience with the king. With Herod.'

Deeply engrossed in debating with himself, Melchior failed to notice when his camel stopped to nibble at a lone thorn bush.

'Why are prophecies so obscure that you only understand them after they come true? Why couldn't the God of the Jews just tell them, 'On such-and-such a day, a virgin will give birth to Me and call me 'God with us.'

'Wait... wait....... He did. He told them when... with a star.'

'Did he tell them what?'

'Yes. A child. A son. Born to a virgin. God with us.'

'Did he tell them where?'

'Maybe. Judah... possibly. We don't know exactly... yet.'

'What else don't we know?'

'Just about everything else.'

'Who knows everything else?'

'God knows. God... the god of the Hebrews... He knows.'

'Would He tell us... would He tell me?'

'Ask.'

'I don't even know His name.'

'Ask'

Melchior framed a question in his mind. The question became a request. The request became a prayer.

He sat a moment longer staring at the distant sea off to their left, then kicked his camel to get it back on the trail. He was falling behind.

The Magi: The Wise Men's Journey To Baby Jesus

Bethlehem

As the forty days of his young wife's sequester drew to a close, the couple prepared to make the short trip to Jerusalem, that the requirements of the Law be met by offering one turtledove as a burnt offering before the Lord, and a second as a sin offering.

Joining a few others for safety on the road, they left their new home at first light. If they didn't linger in the capital, the man hoped to be back the same day. It would be tiring, but they were young.

The Magi: The Wise Men's Journey To Baby Jesus

Gaza

"It's moving," Melchior noted.

Once again, upon reaching Gaza, the caravan had disbanded. The main body, directed by the caravan master, would reconstitute itself with other clients, and continue up the coast, following the trade route north. A few travelers chose to sell their beasts and take ship to distant destinations. Still others, having rested in the relative luxury of Gaza, would turn again east and north on the roads that passed through Marisa, Jerusalem and Jericho, crossed the Jordan River and branched off to the ten cities of the Decapolis and beyond.

For tonight, however, the three scholars were happy to leave their servants camped with the beasts just east of town while they found an innkeeper with a comfortable upper room to let for the night. Having bathed at the public tepidarium, they had gathered on the inn's terraced roof to dine. As the sun set gloriously over the Mediterranean, the three men focused instead on the eastern sky.

"Yes. I believe it is," affirmed Balthasar.

"It is higher now," added Gaspar, "and brighter. Less twinkly."

"I believe what Balthasar meant was that it has shifted its position relative to the other stars," explained Melchior.

"I thought only the planets did that. Could this be one of the planets?"

"No," answered Balthasar. The wine and a full belly had made him mellow, and he continued as if instructing one of his nephews. "The path of each planet is well known. Men have charted their cycles from the days of Noah when the world was remade and the farthest heavens revealed.

"See there," he continued, pointing with his cup, "The brightest one, that is Jupiter at the feet of the right twin of Gemini. Higher up, right in the middle of Taurus, that whitest one is Venus. And the bright point sitting on Taurus' rump is Saturn. Mars has a redish brown, angry color, but it will rise later." Finished with the lesson, he drank from the cup.

"The point is," expounded Melchior, "we can see the five planets and we know where they should be in the night sky, even though they move relative to the stars and constellations. What we do not know is what that star is. It moves, but not like the planets that cross the sky in predictable patterns. It is also unlike a shooting star that flashes across the sky at odd angles and then is gone forever."

"So we have a wandering star," recapped Gaspar, "that appeared on the horizon in the constellation Virgo almost 3 months ago and is now shifted to there." He pointed a bit north of East, to the star that now sat over the distant mountains of Judea. "Which way is Jerusalem from here," he asked?

Both men dropped their eyes from the night sky, instinctively looking to Balthasar for an answer, and found that he had fallen asleep. His cup was resting on the floor at his side, and his chest rose and fell in a gentle rhythm.

They turned at the sound of someone climbing the steps to join them. The innkeeper stepped out onto the roof with a fresh pitcher of wine but Melchior placed his hand over his cup, and the innkeeper understood, bobbed his head and turned to leave this odd trio in peace.

"Can you tell us," Gaspar asked, switching to Greek and speaking slowly and clearly, "Exactly which direction Jerusalem is from here?"

The innkeeper, puzzled at first, moved quietly to set the wine on the table before looking at the eastern horizon.

"There," he said, a note of disgust lacing his words. "The heathen mongrels live up there. See the taller peak? Jerusalem is there." He was dying to know why they had asked such an odd question, but to inquire would be insolent and rude. He paused, hoping they would volunteer an explanation, but when they kept silent, he excused himself. Surely they did not intend to actually go to Jerusalem. Wise men knew to avoid the place. Still, his other guests would be speaking of these odd companions for days, perhaps weeks... and that could be good for his business.

The two royal princes were not silent to keep their intentions secret... they were dumbstruck. The hilltop indicated by the innkeeper was directly under the silent star.

"You will need two camels for each rider," shouted the camel monger, "plus extra beasts for the baggage." He had trotted out as the princes' small caravan approached along the packed earth roadway.

Once the princes had determined among themselves that the road leading to Herod's court was unavoidable, they supposed that they would proceed as they had so far... until accosted by this presumptuous camel merchant. The enterprising opportunist had established a semi-permanent place of business on the outskirts of Marisa, three days out of Gaza, where the road to Jerusalem crossed a stream and the route east to Hebron branched off.

"From here to Jerusalem," the merchant persisted, "the road is all uphill, and it is a very tall mountain. Seventeen hundred cubits."

"He may be right," Balthasar spoke softly to the others. "We should at least consider distributing the baggage to a few other beasts."

"But if we buy more pack animals, we will need more feed, and if we pack more feed and water, we will need more pack animals," countered Gaspar. It had been days since he'd had a good debate, and at this point, any subject open to debate would serve.

"The problem is, we have all the camels we can handle without hiring more men to manage them," pointed out Melchior. Since they had halted next to the stream, he slid off of his camel to help his men refill their water skins. "And if we hire more men," he continued, "we will need to go back to Marisa for more provisions."

Gaspar was thrilled. This debate just kept getting better, with layers upon layers of options, issues and opinions. Managed properly, a good debate could last for days.

"If we rest more," suggested Balthasar, "and climb in manageable stages, it could be done with the beasts we have. We walk more often, shift the heavy water skins to our own mounts through the steeper sections... yes, it can be done."

"Gaspar, that man is admiring what is left of your sedan chair," said Melchior. "Would you be willing to trade it for an extra pack camel?"

"Your camel can carry you up hill, or it can carry your sedan up hill, but not both," added Balthasar. "You choose."

And that settled the matter... and killed the debate.

✧

By midmorning of the next day, they were approaching the foothills of the Judaean mountains. As a show of defense, Balthasar had unpacked a number of weapons from his baggage, handing a short sword and long dagger to Melchior, while keeping a broad scimitar for himself. He even handed a recurve bow to Gaspar, along with a few arrows in a sheath.

"What shall I do with this?" he wanted to know. "I have never used a bow."

"And I hope you never shall," answered the Arab with a crooked smile. "Just sling the bow over your shoulder with the bowstring across your chest. There may be thieves along this hilly trail. The point is, if we look tough and well armed, we will likely not need to use the weapons."

Gaspar had insisted on two camels for his beloved sedan, and the merchant had finally agreed, provided all of the cushions came with it. Gaspar countered that he must keep one fat cushion to ride on, and the man accepted.

Now, as they began the long climb, the two extra pack animals were proving their worth. It was obvious that, sold and resold by the merchant, they had followed this route many times before and needed little guidance. By midday, the two new beasts had been moved to the front of the caravan to set the pace for the other animals and to lead the way.

As planned, they rested the animals more often, and dismounted periodically to walk. That evening, Balthasar suggested an extra measure of salted grain for all of the beasts, and a measure of Gaspar's 'secret' wine supply for each man. While resupplying in Gaza, not all of Gaspar's skins had been filled with water. Drinking it was a pleasant way to help him lighten his load.

The Magi: The Wise Men's Journey To Baby Jesus

Jerusalem

"What a stupid place to build a city," gasped Gaspar. They were making the final steep approaches to the capital on foot to spare the beasts, but planned to unpack their regal attire and mount again before riding through the gates.

"You are thinking like an academic scholar," remarked Balthasar, "not like a warrior. Can you imagine having to bring a besieging army and all of its equipment and supplies up this hill? And then attacking uphill against that wall? It may be a poor choice for agricultural, or even commercial reasons, but as a citadel, it makes perfect sense."

"Also politically," added Melchior. Having spent the last several days ascending the winding trail to the top of this range of mountains, the Persian was inclined to agree with his Indian friend; it was a stupid place to put a city. But he would never concede the point to his friend so easily. Better to make him work for it. "It lies near the center of the kingdom, and at a major crossroads in every direction," he explained.

"Yes," countered Gaspar, "But were the crossroads here first, which made it a tactical place to settle? Or was the city established and *then* the roads came to it? Shall I add it to our list of inquiries?"

"No," the other two answered in unison.

"Let's use the cover of this olive grove to dress," pointed Melchior.
"The animals can rest a moment while we dig out our 'prince' clothes."

It took well over two hours before they were ready to proceed, but Melchior, giving the troop one final inspection, decided it had been worth the effort.

Each camel had been unloaded, brushed down and neatly repacked. The saddle camels and Balthasar's horse were draped in colorfully tasseled silks and resaddled. The princes donned their finest attire, cut in the relatively exotic styles of their various homelands, and their men, getting into the spirit of the charade, brushed their best robes and oiled the tack, the saddles and their own hair until they glistened in the sun.

Balthasar, joining Melchior and Gaspar in the shade of a tree, squinted at the final preparations. "Do you think we are over doing it?"

"We agreed," Melchior reminded him, "that we must make a strong first impression, in order to open the doors that will lead to answered questions."

"Should we hire some musicians?" the Arab asked sarcastically.

"Do you think we could find some?" The sarcasm was lost on Gaspar. It seemed like a reasonable suggestion. Balthasar just looked at him blankly for a moment, then curled his lip and walked off.

"Time to go." Melchior motioned for his people to remount their camels and, with the baggage camels in tow, they formed up in line. As usual, Balthasar took the lead, but for once, all three princes rode together with their colorful caravan trailing out behind.

The walls of Jerusalem had been visible

to them all day, but as they approached the western gate, it became evident that they had become visible, too, as scores of people joined the guards posted along the western walls... but, so far, no one was closing the gate.

"I don't think they know quite what to do about us," muttered Gaspar to the others.

"We are too few to be a threat to them," said Balthasar, "but too... too colorful to be ignored."

Balthasar estimated where an arrow shot from the wall would land and halted short of that point. The other princes came abreast of him and the rest of their company ground to a halt. In the ensuing quiet, the noises of a crowded and bustling city escaped through the still open gateway and over the now crowded walls.

"Do we just ride on in," Melchior asked, "or wait for direc... oh, look there." What looked like a three man emissary was striding from the gate. As they approached, it was evident that the well dressed man in the center was in charge. Upon reaching the regal looking trio, the man bowed deeply, straightened with dignity and spoke what amounted to a long winded and flowery welcome.

Melchior turned to Gaspar, their linguist. "What did he say?"

"I have no idea," he answered, "but it sounded friendly."

Melchior and Balthasar twisted in their saddles to stare in disbelief at their companion.

"What do you mean you don't know? We brought you along to translate for us. How can you not know?"

Gaspar looked stunned and a little hurt. "Translate. Yes, I can translate for you. Give me a document and I can translate it. Aramaic, Greek, Latin, Pashtani, Farsi. I can read thirteen languages besides my own. Most fluently. But I only speak four. And whatever language he just spoke, Hebrew I assume, is not one of them."

The emissary before them looked nervously back and forth as he tried to follow the heated discourse. Not knowing what else to do to placate these young nobles, he bowed again, even more deeply, and repeated his eloquent greeting again... slowly. Upon finishing, he gestured for the three princes to encamp their entourage in the lee of a distinctive nearby hill, that looked shockingly like the face of a human skull.

Dispatching one aide to help the newcomers locate water and firewood, the greeter then sent his other aide to fetch a donkey. When it arrived, he mounted it, sent the second aide to join the first, and motioned for the three princes to follow him into the city. He did not take them into the gate he had exited, however, instead leading them southeast, with the packed city wall on their left. A second, grander gate appeared where two walls joined, and it was here, after months on the road that they finally entered Jerusalem.

Any first impressions they had they wisely kept to themselves. It was time for diplomacy... and caution. The emissary, having dismounted, again bowed, said something pleasant but meaningless to them, and directed them through a second, more ornate gate on their right.

The princes found themselves in a high-walled courtyard entirely leveled and paved with perfectly fit stones in geometric patterns. Before them, an immense marble palace gleamed in the afternoon sunlight. And behind them, the gate closed... with the emissary outside.

The Magi: The Wise Men's Journey To Baby Jesus

Bethlethem

From boyhood, the carpenter had worked long hours developing his skills, saving his earnings and building a good reputation. As a young man, he traded his labor and his skill for materials to build a home, to prepare a place, both for himself and eventually a bride.

Now, all he had built and repaired, saved and prepared all those years was gone. What he could not sell or carry had been left behind in Nazareth. They were starting over with nearly nothing, and they had her child to provide for.

So the carpenter worked long hours.

The Magi: The Wise Men's Journey To Baby Jesus

Jerusalem

"I have a bad feeling," whispered Gaspar. Balthasar's hand moved slowly to the handle of his scimitar. As the son of a nomadic people, he had never liked walls, no matter how shiny. And these walls had tall, fortified guard towers at regular intervals, and guards conspicuously posted along the archers' step built into every wall. And half of those guards were looking in.

"Me, too," confessed the Arab.

"I smell roast lamb," said Melchior, earning him a confused look from his comrades. "And fresh bread... garlic... curry... Can't you smell it?" The others straightened up and sniffed the air. Over the normal pungent aromas of a crowded city, the welcome smell of food wafted on the warm afternoon breeze.

At the top of the palace steps, a well dressed young man with a full beard called to them, then walked out to greet them. No one asked Gaspar what he'd said. Getting no reply from the colorful trio, the bearded fellow motioned for them to walk with him, and proceeded back toward the soaring and ornate palace entry, and into the cool interior.

※

The meal had lasted for hours. All manner of fine foods, pleasingly prepared and skillfully served were set before the princes. Several cups rested within easy reach of each guest, and contained various fresh juices and wines, including pomegranate, honeyed mead, black mulberry, sweet lime, apricot and quince. Course after course paraded before them, followed by music and various entertainments and then more food with no two courses alike.

Well into the evening, the men were escorted to a vast bedroom suite, beautifully appointed and generously supplied with all manner of conveniences. Again wine and platters of finger foods, fruits and sweetened breads were set out for them before they were left for the night. Their bearded host, who had never left their presence or participated in the meal himself, turned at the chamber's door, bowed with a smile and closed the door behind himself.

The three princes stood in silence for a moment, taking in their new surroundings.

"If this is a prison," said Gaspar, "it is a very nice prison."

"I suspect that our effort to impress these folks has had the wrong effect," said Melchior. "They are going to great lengths to impress us... and its working. Just now, I am feeling fairly shabby."

"They did not prepare this enormous palace or this exquisite bed chamber just to impress us," pointed out Balthasar. "I imagine that all regal or royal guests are quartered here. The fact that we are here implies that they have accepted us for royalty, or at least official representatives of royalty."

"Or they are being cautious until they determine otherwise," noted Melchior. "No doubt they've had some of their people among our people all afternoon and evening asking subtle but revealing questions. In fact, quite a number of our servers spoke to me in what sounded like several different languages. Just a few words here and there, like 'how's the soup', 'try the veal', 'have another spicy thing' I suppose."

"They were probing," interjected Gaspar. "There were slaves and servants from around the known world in that room. They were watching for our reaction to their words, whether we understood them or not. No doubt someone put them up to it."

"I recognized some Greek but it was poorly spoken, or so heavily accented as to be almost unintelligible."

"And something that sounded Latin in origin, but I don't speak Latin. I never could conjugate all those verbs."

"So. They were trying to communicate. Wouldn't we? In their place, wouldn't we try to find some common language? It seems harmless."

"This bed looks harmless, too," yawned Gaspar, "and I intend to find out if it is." Draping his robes and other royal finery carelessly over a divan, he collapsed into the cushions of the bed.

The following morning, about midmorning, having been provided a lavish breakfast and an opportunity to wash or bathe, the princes were escorted through the grand palace... and out the back door, to a grandly arcaded garden courtyard of many acres, where several litters awaited, each with four men to transport a prince, lest they grow weary.

Hoisted on the litters, the trio were carried the length of the broad, paved and terraced gardens. The gardens were traced with running streams and clear ponds with bronze founts, and planted with a vast variety of tree, shrub and flower species. Everywhere there was light there was greenery and fruiting plants, both native and exotic.

Small alcoves, arches and delicate arcades contained beautifully crafted bronzes and other sculpted art, much of it painted and decorated with gold leaf. A pair of small antelope watched them pass before returning to tugging leaves from a flowering shrub. Colorful birds and small Asian monkeys chattered from the trees. And at the far end of the gardens, another palace, similar to the first, both in design and grandeur.

At the foot of the steps, the litters were abandoned and the men were escorted through room after room after glorious room, each adorned and decorated with the wealth of a prosperous kingdom, the accumulated wealth of conquered kingdoms, and the meticulous attention of a gifted architect and builder. This place was the culmination of a life's work, the fruit of a brilliant and creative mind driven by ambition and fueled by... by what?

Only the king could have marshaled the resources to fund a building project of this magnitude, thought Melchior, and only a long lived monarch would have the time to see it through to completion. But monarchs did not stay in power through love. They stayed in power through might, or guile, cleverness or ruthlessness. And this king was reported to have killed his own sons, a wife, and his daughters' husbands in order to defend his position, his power, his authority. This spectacular royal compound was testimony to what Herod could do, and what he would do... what he had done... to stave off any threat to his position... real or imagined.

A cold lump made itself known where Melchior's heart beat in his chest. He looked to Balthasar for reassurance, but the look on his own face spoke to the observant Arab prince.

Balthasar nodded just once. "I know. Me, too."

At length, they were lead to a modest room where attendants washed their hands and feet, and anointed their heads and feet with scented oil.

And then they waited. Sweet wine was offered in small gold cups, but they declined. And waited.

Then with a flourish, their bearded escort returned and pressed them to make haste. He ushered them quickly through a small passageway that opened onto a much larger chamber.

There sat the king on a raised dais, surrounded by over twenty members of his court.

Herod rose slowly and looked down upon these nobles whom he did not recognize and had not invited. Once they had arrived at his gate, however, curiosity compelled him to discover why.

He had immediately instructed two of his personal guards to assume the clothing and mannerisms of junior aides and dispatched them to snoop about the visitors' camp under the guise of being helpful. He sent his steward to welcome the three noblemen, with the intent of separating them from their men. The steward then escorted these strangers directly into the confines of his palatial citadel, but without them viewing the city itself. Or its defenses.

To give himself time to debrief his two spies, the king ordered a lavish banquet be prepared immediately and that these men be treated like kings... or at least the royal emissaries of kings.

Balthasar was the first to remember his manners, placing his right hand over his heart and bowing in the manner of his people. Herod acknowledged with a slow, deep nod, never taking his eyes off of the trio. Gaspar, too, bowed in turn with his palms together over his breast bone, in the manner common to his land, and received a solemn nod in return. Melchior, placed both hands over his heart, and as he bowed swept them down and away at his sides with his palms forward... and received an unsmiling nod.

And then... silence. No one, it seemed, was prepared to initiate even simple dialog, the king because his spies had discovered nothing informative or remotely threatening in the visitors' camp, and the princes because they had hoped to avoid an official audience entirely.

After several uncomfortable minutes had lapsed, the bearded steward ushered in two men, one wearing a merchant's apron and a seriously frightened expression, while the other wore little more than chains. The merchant dropped prostrate before Herod and, aside from an occasional tremor, just lay there. But the silent king neither looked at those men, nor acknowledged their presence. It was the steward who spoke first, addressing the princes directly.

"Herod, king of Judea, Idumaea, Galilee, Samaria and Peraea bids you welcome," he declared in Hebrew, then muttered an instruction to the man on the floor, who rose only to his knees, and without looking up from the floor, translated it into something else, though the princes had no clue what he'd said. It was the prisoner who surprised them by speaking the local Greek dialect they had heard in Gaza.

"King Herod of Judea, Idumaea, Galilee, Samaria and Peraea makes you welcome."

Before they could respond in kind, the steward spoke again.
"The great King hopes your travels have been both pleasant and profitable, and trusts that his staff has made your stay restful."

The merchant thought for a moment before translating, and the prisoner, too, in his limited Greek.

"The King hopes your travels are pleasing and profitable, and your visit is rested." Then all the king's men waited.

When neither of his companions spoke up, Melchior answered, recalling diplomatic niceties from his own king's court, and speaking slowly to give the man in chains a chance to absorb it.

"May the king live long," he said. "May

the king live forever. And may all his days be as pleasant as our stay here has been." He nodded a brief bow to indicate that, for the moment he was finished.

Again the court waited as the impromptu interpreters passed along what they'd heard.

By the looks of confusion and consternation Melchior was getting, he had to assume that something had been lost in the translation. Quickly, he made a second attempt, this time keeping it simpler and shorter. "Thank you for the food and wine." Followed by a small nod.

This time the prisoner looked more confident, the merchant on the floor did not hesitate, and the looks of confusion dissipated.

"That one must have gotten through," muttered Gaspar. "Say something else." Melchior considered what to... ah.

"If it pleases the king --" he waited for the translation, "make yourselves comfortable --", again the short wait, "and I will tell you our story." This met with obvious relief and anticipation, but all eyes looked to Herod for his consent. With the slightest nod to his steward, the king returned to his padded seat and settled in. Only then did his councilors and advisors call for seats to be brought in, and the steward beckon for seats to be brought for the princes.

It took a few minutes to get everyone settled but Melchior could see that he had made the right choice. Everyone likes a story. While Balthasar and Gaspar were seated, Melchior remained standing and began his tale, again speaking slowly and in short, manageable portions.

"We three travelers -- are the sons of kings -- each in his own country -- My companions on this journey are -- Balthasar, Prince of Arabia -- and Prince Gaspar, from the courts of India -- And my named is Melchior, Prince of Persia --

"We have come from afar -- through distant lands -- by river and sea -- over mountain passes -- and desert sand -- To the court of the great king -- we have come -- This is our story." He had his audience primed for a long tale of adventure and hardship. And for the next 2 hours he gave it to them... with a few embellishments. Some to make their adventure more exciting. Some to obscure certain facts.

Melchior told of the many years he and his friends had been away from their homes in a distant land, but not that they had been students surrounded by the comforts of Alexandria. He spoke of seeing a new star in the east, but did not clarify that it was the star, and not themselves, that was in the east. He recounted how a learned magi from the east had recalled an ancient prophecy regarding a star, but did not explain that that magi was Gaspar.

"The prophesy foretold -- that a star -- would herald the birth -- of a king in Judaea."

Suddenly, Herod sat up just a little straighter, and the members of his court froze. Melchior noticed the subtle, but sudden change, but could see no option but to continue.

"So we three travelers -- determined to journey here -- to congratulate the great king -- and to honor -- the new born prince."
Melchior paused, but no one spoke or moved. Nervous eyes flitted between the king and this guest, awaiting some indicator from the

king or his steward. Melchior, searching for a means to diffuse the sudden tension, decided it was time to plead ignorance.

"If it pleases the great king -- our three kings -- would like to know -- if the new star overhead -- is the star of the prophesy -- and if so -- where shall we go -- to see the child -- and to honor him?"

At last the king spoke from his throne, addressing his steward, who relayed it to the princes through the merchant and the prisoner.

"The king thanks you for coming -- and for entertaining him -- with your adventures -- but regrets to inform you -- that no such child exists -- however -- he will consult his astronomers -- concerning the star -- and his historians -- regarding any relevant prophecies."

Herod spoke again, this time addressing Melchior directly.

"Return to your encampment -- outside the gates of our city -- and rest while we pursue these inquiries -- My stewards will summon you when all is ready."

At this point the steward moved to

escort them out of the king's presence, but the three princes, remembering the lessons of their youth, took the time to bow formally before departing.

※

The trio remained silent until they had ridden well beyond the city gates. "Well done, Melchior," the Arab murmured. He could see his friend's hands tremoring and his jaws clenching. Having stood firm in the court of a potentially hostile monarch for hours, now that the immediate danger had passed, the Persian prince was exhausted. The adrenaline that had fueled his composure was draining away to be replaced by... what?

"What you need is a cup of wine," said Balthasar. "Perhaps two."

"Or twelve," added Gaspar.

"And some food. Not that rich, fancy stuff either. Bread, meat, cheese, dates."

"And more wine."

Melchior neither spoke or looked to his friends. Upon arriving at camp, he dismounted his camel, entered his tent, saw that his bedding had been prepared and lay trembling until sleep finally took over.

※

"That man has been pruning the same tree for two hours." The student princes gathered about a small fire to ward off the next morning's chill and discuss their options. They had posted some of their men to watch the camp through the night, and now it was apparent that they, too, were being watched.

"Yes. And the shepherd on that slope has let half his flock wander off while he watches our camp," observed Balthasar. "No doubt the king has watchers stationed all about us. I've spotted four others so far. These may be the few we are allowed to discover as a warning, while others are more cleverly hidden nearby."

"Warning?" asked Gaspar. "What kind of warning?"

"A reminder not to wander off, until the king gives his leave," said Balthasar.

"And not to go snooping about, either," added Melchior. "Did you notice how neatly we were escorted to the king without actually entering the city itself? We were allowed to see only that which Herod wished us to see. Nothing more."

"So what shall we do?" asked Gaspar.

"We wait," answered Balthasar, and for a while, each was lost in his own thoughts.

Balthasar's steward arranged a light morning meal but otherwise the three were left alone. Melchior ate little and refused wine. His stomach would not allow it. He hated waiting.

Supposedly, Herod's astronomers, astrologers, historians, priests and magi were even then scouring their records, seeking references to the star, the ancient prophecies, the coming birth of a king, and would advise their king accordingly. But Melchior, a scholar himself, understood that research like this requires time. Lots of time. Dusty, half-forgotten old scrolls, stored away in earthen jars deep in the corners of disused library cellars, would be resurrected and scrutinized for the first time in centuries, their brittle edges crumbling to the lightest touch. Time. It could takes several days... or weeks. Melchior hated waiting.

But it wasn't the Hebrew king, or his scribes, that Melchior was waiting on. It was their god. If the god of the Hebrews intended to answer his question, his prayer, then the answer should come soon. Must come soon. But he hated waiting.

Through the day, the men of the camp watched the patient guards watching them. And they all waited.

✦

Balthasar, having slept through the warm afternoon, rose early the next day, the sky yet dark as he slipped quietly from his grand tent. Only a hint of the coming day graced the eastern horizon. He loved this time of quiet, this time to be alone.

Without thinking, his eyes were drawn to the still bright stars above. The same stars that had captured his imagination as a boy growing up in a desert land. The calm, clear air of a desert morning allowed his clear young eyes to see every tiny point of light. It was a fascination that he had never outgrown.

"Good morning."

Balthasar nearly choked as he spun about to see a shadow sitting beside a cold fire pit and smiling at his reaction.

"My apologies, my friend," Melchior added, "for disturbing your peaceful moment, but I did not want... Are you well?"

"You could stop a man's heart like that," the Arab managed to gasp. Bent over with his hands on his knees for support, he strove to recover from the blast of adrenaline his friend had caused.

"If you ever... its a good thing my weapons are still in the tent, or I might have taken your head off before I recognized your voice. Stop laughing."

Melchior made an effort to hide the smile he could not avoid, but did stop laughing for his friend's pride's sake.

"That looked painful. If you have hurt yourself..." He rose to join his friend.

"If I have hurt myself," Balthasar grumbled, straightening slowly, "then it is your fault. Why are you up, anyway? You look terrible."

Melchior, placing one hand on the Arab prince's shoulder, pointed to the southern sky, just above the hilly horizon. "That's why." The bright morning star was suspended just above the hills of Judah. "We've been so focused on where the star appears each evening that we've taken no notice of where it settles at the dawn."

Balthasar considered this for a moment. "What is south from here?"

"I do not know."

The Magi: The Wise Men's Journey To Baby Jesus

Bethlehem

Nothing moves as quickly as gossip, and the tale the shepherds had told, of angels and heavenly hosts announcing the long awaited Christ, had exploded throughout the surrounding countryside like an ohmer of beads dropped on a stone floor.

The arrival of visitors knocking at the inn's door asking to see 'the babe' was, at first, a source of some pride for the innkeeper and his wife, but quickly turned to an annoyance as the curious and skeptical paraded through. They were mostly locals who spent little or no money at the inn, but managed to interrupt the busy couple without apology. Eventually, they posted one of their granddaughters at the door to direct 'well wishers' to the carpenter's small house on the edge of town.

The Magi: The Wise Men's Journey To Baby Jesus

Jerusalem

Late on the eleventh day, the bearded steward appeared in their camp but dressed in the attire of a merchant or craftsman, and escorting a stooped little man in common clothes. He recognized Melchior and directed the little man to deliver a message.

"The Great King is prepared to meet with you. You will meet this man," he indicated the steward, "by the city gate when the star is higher than that highest tower. Only you three. Come on foot." He then turned away and the two visitors melted into the growing shadows of evening.

※

After dinner, when the star finally cleared the tower, and the noises of the city around it had died for the night, the princes, with common cloaks to cover their regal robes, casually walked away from camp with only two armed servants as escort. As they neared the gate, they could see the lone steward waiting, and Balthasar instructed his men to remain at a distance unless called upon.

Passing through the city gate quickly, their guide led them by the same route to the same entry court before the palace where they had dined several nights before. Assuming they were to pass again through that palace and on to the next, the princes were a bit surprised to hear a voice speak from the shadows behind them. Herod himself stood in the shadows of the palace wall with only the stooped old man kneeling off to his left. Stunned by this unorthodox meeting place, the princes neglected all protocol and simply waited on the king to speak. When he did, the little man translated for him.

"My scribes and astrologers -- have found only a vague reference -- to a prophecy -- regarding a child -- born to the line of our King David -- who reigned hundreds of years ago. -- There was no mention -- of a star in that prophecy." As the translator fell silent, and Herod looked at them expectantly, the student princes tried to grasp what the king intended them to do with this new information. As their spokesman, Melchior thought that he should say something. But what? He began speaking, hoping that inspiration would come to him as he spoke.

"We are honored -- by the Great King -- and thank him -- for taking time -- to assist us in our quest.-- We can now report -- to our respective monarchs -- that a great and benevolent king exists in Judah -- but that the prophecies uncovered -- have not here been fulfilled.-- If it please the Mighty King, -- we will depart in the morning -- and remember our visit to your courts -- with fond appreciation."

'There,' thought Melchior, 'if Herod wants rid of us, I have given him the opportunity to say good bye and send us back down this hill.' But Herod's look of expectation had now turned to consternation. He had not gotten the response he expected. The response he required.

"You have traveled a long way -- from your homes in the east.-- Can you tell me how long ago -- you first sighted the star?"

Melchior had to quickly remember from the twisted tale he'd told of their travels, about how long...

"It has been almost two years -- since the star was first reported -- in my country. -- We assumed -- that it had been visible here -- for two years as well." Melchior could feel the king's eyes burning into his own and hoped that the lie was accepted.

Herod contemplated the translation, scratching absently at his bearded chin before replying.

"Such a shame," he said, "to search so long -- without searching just a little further. -- According to the prophesy -- the child you seek would be born -- in the town of Bethlehem. -- It is my wish -- that you three go and search for the boy, -- and having found him, -- report back to me, -- so that I may come there -- and worship him, also."

This seemed like a reasonable request, so Melchior replied, "It shall be as the Great King suggests.-- If we may refill our water skins in the morning, -- and purchase provisions at your market, -- we will surely depart by midday."

This time the steward spoke for the king.

"Such provisions as you require -- will be provided at your camp in the morning. -- You are our guests."

"Your hospitality is no doubt legendary -- among your people and all the lands. -- But there is one other thing that we require." Again, Melchior noted the shrewd and penetrating look from the king.

"Where," asked Melchior, "is Bethlehem?"

※

Once back at their camp, the trio checked on their people, confirmed that none of Herod's folk were nearby and retired to the Arab's spacious tent, but not to sleep.

"Am I the only one who thinks that was too easy?" asked Gaspar.

"Something is not quite right," confirmed Melchior.

"Several things," added Balthasar. "First, the King of Judah claims they know of only vague references to a prophecy regarding the birth of a future king of Judah while Gaspar stumbled across a copy of it in Egypt.

"Second, they claim to know nothing of the star, yet the star is central to the whole prophecy, and any astronomer over the age of three can see that star and know it shouldn't be there.

"Thirdly, that star appeared suddenly, yes, but suddenly everywhere. The heavens move about us and can be viewed from anywhere you travel. If we saw it two years ago, which we didn't, then they saw it two years ago, which they didn't. He should have kno... oh, wait. He didn't know. His astrologers didn't... they knew, and they didn't tell him.

"Bad news can get the messenger killed," noted Gaspar, thinking again of the sharp, pointy stakes. "And if they didn't tell him about the star, or about the prophecies..."

"Then his people probably know all about the prophecies but haven't told him everything."

All three minds were focused on the implications. And all three came to the same conclusion.

✴

"May I leave my tent here?" Balthasar inquired the next morning through the stooped translator. "Since we are planning to be back here in a matter of days, I see no point in packing it up and taking it along."

The bearded steward smiled, and agreed. Leaving such a large tent behind made perfect sense. No, it would not be in anyone's way there, and he offered to post a man to guard it until the princes returned. It also affirmed to him that the foreigners were actually going along with the king's plan, and intended to return to Jerusalem before continuing on their way.

He smiled. He would have good news for his monarch.

✴

It still took over an hour to redistribute the remaining baggage to include four of the five 'tent' camels. The fifth was loaded with the promised provisions. The steward delivered just enough food and water for three days; four at most, and no feed for the beasts. The king had provided just enough to get them there and back, nothing more.

By midmorning, the lead camels of the small caravan had followed Balthasar's horse onto the road south. Bethlehem, they were instructed, was a very small place of no consequence. It lay along this narrow road that followed the spine of the Judaean mountains. On level terrain, the six mile trip should have taken as many hours, perhaps less, but this rough mountain trail insured they would not arrive before sunset.

✦

Negotiating the hazardous mountain road in the dark was not an option. By the failing light they could see the rooftops of a village not a mile off, but dared not proceed until morning light, and so prepared a hasty camp astride the road itself.

"The cool night air feels good,"

remarked Balthasar absently.

"This mountain air will be very cool by morning," noted Melchior.

"How can you two talk about the weather at a time like this?" Gaspar wanted to know. Melchior leaned closer to whisper.

"If I were Herod, I would consider sending at least one or two spies to shadow us. And if I were a spy, I would consider using the cover of darkness to creep close to the camp and listen to conversations."

Gaspar did not take long to imagine what that could lead to. "It's a good thing we have our warm robes," he said a bit too loudly, "since it will be so cold."

Despite the mixed stands of trees among the hills, little firewood remained after the women of the area had gathered dead branches to cook and heat their homes, but it was a mild evening with no prospect for rain this late in the season, so the princes were content with their robes.

Eventually, their attention turned again to the star. It had risen again shortly after dusk, and without a fire or bright moon to ruin their night vision, the men scanned the starry night in silence, until one by one they slipped away to rest.

※

"Don't cut my head off," whispered Melchior. Balthasar had risen early again and Melchior rolled to his feet to join him. "Do you see what I see?" he asked. Balthasar simply nodded without turning or speaking. Through the night, the tableau of heavenly lights had rotated until, in the still morning sky just before first light, the new star had come to rest over Bethlehem. And just as it settled low over a single rooftop on the edge of town, the eastern sky was washed in the blood red first light of the coming dawn. Balthasar raised his hand to point, tracing a finger along the ruby band of morning light.

"That is what I saw," murmured Balthasar, breaking his silent vigil, "I had a dream... and I think I understand its meaning." But before he could explain, a disturbance in the camp drew their attention. Rushing toward raised voices, they discovered Gaspar writhing on the ground, pinned there by two of his men.

"What are you two doing?" demanded the Arab.

"Our master woke us with his screaming, Lord Prince," one of them explained. Gaspar, still visibly upset, had struggled to his knees and was scrubbing at his forearms with loose dirt while begging for water. Melchior pressed by the others and, grabbing Gaspar up by the front of his robe, hugged him tight and spoke into his ear.

"All is well, Gaspar," he said softly, as if reassuring a child. "You are safe, you are okay. Your parents are okay." As Gaspar continued to struggle, Melchior cast about for something he could say to... "Your sister is okay." That last assurance seemed to break the spell and Gaspar stopped flailing about.

"All is well," the Persian repeated. "You've had a bad dream. Nothing more. Only a dream." Slowly he released his shattered friend but, for the moment, kept a gentle grip on the man's sleeves. He could feel Gaspar begin to shake as the tension drained away. Speaking to one of Gaspar's men, Melchior called for wine and a cup of strong drink was brought.

By the time the camp had settled again, the sun was breaking over the hilltops to wash the surrounding slopes and terraced fields with morning light.

"I did not know Gaspar had a sister," noted Balthasar.

"I don't," Gaspar muttered from the rock he was seated on. "Only brothers." He sipped again from the wine, then set it aside. "Melchior knows this." What he wanted was to fetch water with which to wash his hands and arms, but did not yet trust his shaky legs.

"Gaspar has a logical mind," explained Melchior. "Mentioning a sister forced him to think. Forced him to focus on whether or not he had a sister. It was a simple trick to bring him back to reality."

"You call this reality?" chuckled the Arab. "We are following a star to find a boy child, born to a virgin, in a little town even the locals cannot find on a map, with only centuries old prophecies to guide us. Prophecies written in an archaic script that no one reads anymore. This is reality?"

"I read archaic script," grumbled Gaspar, looking up for the first time.

"There. See? He makes my point."

Melchior knew then that all would be okay. His best friends were squabbling again.

But there was no time for that. The sun was up and their destination was literally in sight again, less than an hour's walk away. Even less if they...

"Leave the camp here," he said aloud. "Let's leave the camp here. The men can stay here, too, to guard the camp and see to the beasts." As the thoughts came to him he spoke. "It will be much faster for the three of us to go alone, and less frightening for the town. Compared to that little place, we look like an invading army. They may run to the hills or try to hide the child king."

"We three can put on our prince outfits while our camels are prepared," added Balthasar, already turning toward his personal baggage pack. "I can be ready in... hey, you two," he said, indicating Gaspar's men, "change your master from those dirty travel clothes to his good robes. But not his hat." With that, he was off to clean up. They must make a good impression. The parents of the child king must be royalty.

The Magi: The Wise Men's Journey To Baby Jesus

Bethlehem

Caravans passed by from time to time. But Bethlehem lay in a tight vale, down a rock strewn slope off to one side of the road, too small and too poor to be of much use or interest to the merchants, tradesmen, diplomats, royal messengers, pilgrims or priests traveling to or from Jerusalem. And with only one small spring to provide the community with water, they had little to spare. So the caravans passed by.

The younger daughter, posted at the doorway of the inn to deflect the dwindling stream of curious gawkers, was not alarmed to see the three well dressed travelers approaching along the road to Hebron, until they turned off that road, taking the packed earth trail winding down the slope toward her.

She glanced about to assure herself that she was not alone, and spotted several other folks about their daily chores, mostly various distant relatives too old to work the fields or mine stones from the local quarry. Turning again, she watched as the splendid trio rode into town, tall on their camels in the morning light... and stopped... and looked at her.

With mouth hanging open, she did what she had been told to do. Without hesitation, she pointed right at the carpenter's little house. The three kings, for surely they must be kings, followed her slender finger to where a doorway stood open. The kings did not speak, but one of them faced her again, smiled gently, placed both hands over his heart and slowly nodded a bow to her. *'Thank you'*. Her trembling knees failed, and as he turned his camel toward the open door down the street, she plopped down on her behind against the door to the inn.

What little activity remained in town this late in the morning was no match for the colorful three-camel parade that moved slowly down the main street. Dusty floors, weedy gardens and dirty diapers could wait. As the "kings" progressed, others helpfully pointed to the carpenter's house, lest they get lost along the way. A few, not knowing what else to do, knelt or bowed, but no one presumed to speak.

Arriving at the house, Balthasar looked about anxiously like there must be some mistake, but Melchior bade his camel kneel down and dismounted. Gaspar, still shaken from the morning, made no move to follow.

As Melchior stood before the open doorway, a small cloud of dust escaped over the door sill, followed by the bare feet of the young girl who had swept it out. With two more whisks of her short handled broom fashioned from native pine boughs, she straightened, tucked a loose strand of hair behind her ear... and gaped into the face of an unexpected visitor.

Her dark eyes widened as they flicked from one royal visitor to another, and her chin dropped as her lips formed the unspoken word, *'Oh'*. Taking half a step back, she rested one calloused hand against the door frame for support as she stood under the door's rugged lintel. A second camel knelt to allow its master down, and she suspected in that moment why these men, like the shepherds and so many others, had come. As the first king placed both his palms over his heart and bowed, she knew. Beckoning with hand motions, she invited him, them, into her home.

The third king, aided by his friends, stepped away from his mount, and the resplendent trio passed under the nail scarred lintel and into the confines of the single room that a humble, hardworking carpenter had prepared for his loved ones. As they looked on, the girl gently lifted an infant from his bed in a box. He was awake anyway, and as she turned him to face his visitors, he refocused from her familiar face to theirs... and as infants often do, he smiled a big, toothless grin at them.

The girl could read the unspoken question in the young king's face, and on impulse gently handed him the babe. Melchior stood very still, holding the child who looked up at him and burbled softly, happily. He turned to Gaspar, got a nod from the girl, and offered him the child to hold, but the dark prince tucked his hands behind his back and shook his head. He did not trust himself, even if the child's mother did.

Balthasar came alongside Gaspar and accepted the babe from Melchior. Cradling the boy with one arm, his broad hand supporting its head, he took Gaspar's hand in his and raised it to the child, who with one chubby hand grasped Gaspar's little finger, and with the other caught hold of the gold pendant hanging about Balthasar's neck. Balthasar laughed as the child tugged the bright ornament. And Gaspar wept.

As Melchior retrieved the babe, Balthasar slipped the gold pendant and its gold chain from his neck and offered both to the child's mother.

"I suspect you will be needing this," he said, though he knew she would not understand the words. When she hesitated to take it from him, he gently took her small hand in his and placed the heavy pendant in her palm.

Melchior, sensing they had tarried long enough, passed the boy back to the girl who took him one-handed with practiced ease. The strand of her hair had escaped again and the child reached out for it. Setting the boy back in his improvised cradle, the girl turned again to the three kings, and found that they were kneeling, and the shorter king's silent tears were spotting her freshly swept dirt floor.

"You have not revealed your name to us," spoke Melchior for them all, "but you have revealed your son to us. Your signs you have made known to us, even before we knew to ask. Can any man wonder why these people need only one god. May the Lord bless and keep these his people to the measure that they remember and honor You."

Gaspar stood suddenly and rushed from the house.

"We must do something for these people," said Balthasar, looking about the cramped little house. "For this child." Even as he spoke, Gaspar returned with a small, well made pouch from his saddle bag. Even closed, the heady, resinous aroma of murrha escaped the pouch to sweeten the windowless room. Each hardened nodule of murrha was worth a laborer's annual income, and the small pouch was full.

The Arab had given a gold pendant and chain but now took a small knife and slit the lining of his belt to reveal the small gold coins hidden within. From these he selected half and laid them with the murrha.

Melchior, seeing the wisdom and

practicality of their gifts, remembered the expensive but light weight olibanum he'd purchased in Alexandria. Known in the west as frankincense, it could be redeemed for eight or even ten times the value of murrha.

Reaching in at the neck of his shirt, Melchior drew out a small glass vial suspended from a simple leather thong about his neck. With a tug he broke the thong and held the tiny vial in his palm. He removed the carved wooden stopper just for an instant, and the escaping essence suffused the room with the masking perfume of the sepulcher.

The tiny nodules of hardened gum were worth a fortune... but not in this little town. In fact there was no market here for any of their extravagant gifts. But like the others, Melchior suspected that the girl and child should leave soon. Very soon. And so should they.

※

Not knowing how to effectively convey their concerns to the girl, the princes retreated back toward their camp above Bethlehem. Once clear of the village, Melchior broke their silence.

"I dreamt last night that I had discovered a wealth of hidden treasure. A fortune in gold and colored gemstones. And I rejoiced, gathering my friends about me and rejoicing in my great fortune. But as I displayed the great horde for all to see, the gold turned to bread and that bread turned to flesh. Likewise, the basins and bowls of colored gems turned first to water, then to wine, and finally to blood. I have no idea what it all means."

"What did you see, Balthasar," asked Melchior, as they rode slowly back toward camp. "You said you had been awakened by a dream. What did you see."

"I do not usually remember dreams. But this one has lingered on my mind all day. In my dream a scepter plunged like a lance into flesh, and the rising sun was red with blood... so much blood. Three times the sun rose and three times the scepter struck it red with blood." The Arab was not sure of his interpretation of the dream, but shared it anyway. "I think the three sunrises are just that, three days. The scepter represents a king, perhaps Herod, and the blood... may be ours. Three dreams, three sunrises, three of us. But I cannot be sure. I do not know. But I feel... something is... I sense great danger. It is time to run."

"Or," speculated Melchior, "it could be the babe who is in danger. Perhaps it is his blood you see."

"No," said Gaspar, staring blankly at the road ahead. The first word he had spoken since morning. "It is the blood of many children, many babes." He shuddered and new tears broke free to run tracks down his dark cheeks. "I heard them. The cries of the children cut short, the weeping and bitter tears of the mothers, the fathers. I heard them. And there was blood. Innocent blood, dripping from the blade in my hand. Blood on my arms. So much blood. I could not drop the blade. And I could not wash off the blood."

Melchior grabbed at Gaspar's hands. With his nails he had begun scraping at his own forearms, to remove the blood he could still see in his mind, and the scraping had produced the blood he feared. "I can smell it," he said. "I can smell the blood." Melchior and Balthasar traded a concerned look.

※

"He met with us in secret to avoid being suspected himself."

"And he sent us to confirm the prophecy and to find the child for him."

"When we had located the child, he could send an assassin, pin the blame on us, plead ignorance and have us..."

"We need to get out of this country."

"I will miss that tent," muttered Balthasar, but going back to Jerusalem was not an option.

"You can buy another. Pack quickly. It is time to go."

※

Within the hour, the camp had been reduced to one cold fire pit, various holes in the dirt where stakes had held tents or camels, and the shallow latrine the men had dug the day before.

Since the road north led to Herod's gates, the well rested caravan turned south. They would have to go home another way.

As they passed the little town, Melchior could see a little girl standing before the inn and he raised his hand to her, a silent 'good bye'. He could not tell if she had raised a slender arm to wave back. His eyes were then drawn to the tiny house on the edge of town where another girl nursed her baby boy, mended her husband's clothes, prepared the food he'd earned, and then sat on the floor by her son's bed as he slept, and marveled at the path her life had taken since she had spoken those simple words: 'Be it unto me...'

"Lord God," Melchior pleaded softly under his breath, "we have done what we can. The rest is up to you." He thought he should say more, but upon reflection decided to leave the details to... "Will I ever know your name?"

"It is time I had a son," proclaimed Balthasar, from the head of the column. Having resupplied in Hebron two days later, the small caravan turned west and south, circling back toward the relative safety of Gaza. From that port city, a man could embark to all of the known world.

"A strong and handsome son. Who likes horses," Balthasar added.

"You don't even have a wife yet," countered Gaspar.

"Then I shall get one. Maybe two. Then I shall have a son."

"I will marry, too. I will find a good girl once I return to Alexandria and we shall marry and have a son. Several sons."

"Not as many sons as me."

"What do you care? You will be back in Arabia by then."

And once again, Melchior knew that all would be well.

Your questions answered by author Ken Proctor.

Were there really three kings named Melchior, Gaspar and Balthazar?

The Bible story, recorded in the second chapter of the book of Matthew, does not give these men's names. However, according to the Encyclopedia Britannica, Western Christian tradition and early literature do preserve these names, or minor variations of them, as the real names of the three "wise men", or magi, who followed a star to the little town of Bethlehem, in Judea. Other ancient records provide somewhat different, or very different, names, but always three names. It is highly unlikely, though, that these men traveled alone. No doubt they were accompanied by servants, and linked their entourage with others along the way.

I thought the wise men came from the east?

Again, scripture is silent on either their national origins or their point of origin. Tradition and the names themselves, however, suggest that Melchior may have been Persian, Gaspar from India, and Balthasar (or Balthazar) from Arabia or possibly Babylonia. How such an unlikely trio got together is unknown, unless, as my story suggests, they began at a common point of origin, Alexandria, and knew each other there.

Could they really have come east from Alexandria, Egypt, rather than from east to west?

Years ago, I heard it suggested that if they saw the star in the east, they must have been in the west. If you look at a map or globe, you find that Alexandria, the greatest repository of records and learning at that time (or ever) is due west of Bethlehem. The question then arises, if they saw the star rising in the east, was it them in the east seeing the star, or the star itself rising from the eastern horizon? Besides, where else in the ancient world would three guys without kingdoms to run get together to dig through ancient prophesies about astrological signs?

What do we know about the Library at Alexandria? Were there really more than one?

Much has been written on this subject and is readily available. The relevance to our story is that due to the extensive archives stored at the multiple libraries in Alexandria, particularly the Royal Library, scholars from all the known world converged here. Knowledge, after all, is power. Or, at least, the key to wealth.
By law, every vessel entering the Port of Alexandria was required to surrender every document they carried. The library scribes produced a copy of each, returning the copy to the traders while keeping the

originals for their archives.

It is entirely likely that all manner of books of law and prophecy found their way into the vast storerooms lining the walls, including very early copies of the relevant Hebrew texts printed in Aramaic, or translated into Greek. All was lost however when the city was sacked and the libraries burned and/or destroyed. No one is quite sure when or by whom since historical accounts vary depending on who won and who wrote them.

Did the star really appear in the constellation Virgo, or did you make that up?

According to star charts that can be accurately calculated back thousands of years, at the time of Christ's birth Virgo was low on the eastern horizon. Therefore, from Alexandria, a new star poised over Bethlehem would appear to be in the belly of Virgo, the Virgin. That discovery shocked me, too.

(Further research uncovered a wealth of confusing information in this regard, much of it spinning off into astrology and interpretations that I neither understand or care to condone so I've listed none of them as references.)

Did the Magi really find Jesus in a house? I thought they found him away in a manger?

The Bible is clear. The shepherds found the babe

wrapped in swaddling clothes and lying in a manger just as the angel said. The Magi, however, found the child and his mother in a house maybe months after the shepherds' visits. Some suggest that since Herod ordered every boy child in Bethlehem under the age of three slain, it might have been years later.

Was Bethlehem really little because there was only one little spring to provide water?

Yes. The book of Samuel reports there was a single well there during King David's lifetime, but I've seen an old photo in a book (which I cannot now relocate) that shows a tiny natural spring of fresh water still visible at that time in the rocky slope just outside of town. The caption notes that this precious but limited water supply is why Bethlehem was one of the first settlements in the region but also why it remained small. Archeologists have uncovered several ancient cisterns carved deep into the bedrock the town sits on, giving the inhabitants the ability to store rainfall and any excess from the spring. These cisterns may be the well Samuel was referring to, centuries before the Magi got there.

Do we really know how the magi got from Alexandria to Bethlehem?

The ancient trade routes in the Middle East and northern Africa are pretty well known. Some are still visible by satellite, today. A quick look at those maps pretty much defines for us the most logical and direct route from Alexandria to Jerusalem, either overland or by sea. Both routes lead to the port city of Gaza and from there it is a fairly straight shot up mountain trails to Jerusalem and then south to Bethlehem. Since they didn't want to return to Jerusalem, the only other road available to The Magi lead south to Hebron. Where they went after that isn't known.

Were the people of Gaza really hostile to their Israelite neighbors?

The Philistines, of Philistia (a loose confederation of city states on the coast around where the Gaza strip is today), and the descendants of God's people, who returned from Egypt with Moses after almost 450 years, were constantly at each other's throats. Remember the story of David and Goliath? Goliath was from Gath, a city at the north end of Philistine rule and a champion among the Philistine warriors. Even when Christ was born centuries later, animosity remained between these people.

Why would the Magi give them gold, frankincense and myrrh?

In many cultures a gift was customary when approaching royalty. As the story goes, these three items of great value were relatively small, light and easily transported. Whether the three "kings" intended these as items as gifts all along or were simply drawn from the resources they had on hand for travel expenses, we do not know. In all accounts, these three gifts are mentioned. Their names may be muddled by history, but three gifts remain constant. These valuable, precious gifts would also allow the young mother, her husband, and her child to flee Herod at a moment's notice.

Did Joseph and Mary really flee south to Egypt?

We know they did, probably following the same route as the three Magi: south to Hebron, west to the coastal road, and by caravan south across the Wadi El-Arish (Mizraim) and into Egypt where Herod's agents could not follow. When word of Herod's death reached them there a few years later, they were directed back north. Herod's son still reigned in Judea, however, so as a precaution, Joseph settled them in a quiet little backwater town, Nazareth.

About Ken Proctor

As an author and researcher Ken Proctor brings depth, meaning, and understanding by restoring historical, geographical, and cultural context to the Bible stories you thought you knew. Incorporating more of the historical record and recent archeological discoveries, Ken shares with his readers, as Paul Harvey used to say, "the rest of the story." Ken works from his home in Vancouver, Washington, in a cramped little office that resembles a museum's back store room, surrounded by fossils, relics, old books and crusty antiques.

**KenProctorAuthor.com
360-909-1110**

Made in the USA
Lexington, KY
23 September 2017